MYSTERY AT THE OLD MINE

by Katie Parker
illustrated by Dylan Gibson

a Capstone company — publishers for children

Engage Literacy is published in the UK by Raintree.
Raintree is an imprint of Capstone Global Library Limited, a company incorporated in England and Wales
having its registered office at 264 Banbury Road, Oxford, OX2 7DY – Registered company number:
6695582

www.raintree.co.uk

Editorial credits
Erika L. Shores, editor; Cynthia Della-Rovere, designer; Katy LaVigne, production specialist

21 20 19 18 17
10 9 8 7 6 5 4 3 2 1
Printed and bound in India.

Mystery at the Old Mine

ISBN: 978 1 4747 4704 2

CONTENTS

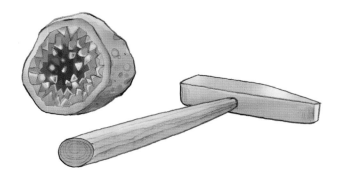

Chapter One
FIELD TRIP

"We're here!" Raj called. Their bus had just pulled up to the Torpie Family Mine.

Mia, Ari and Jez followed him off the bus. The science club was on a field trip to a gold mine that had closed long ago. Today, people came to dig for rocks and gems, like emeralds and amethysts. Whatever they found, they could keep.

TORPIE
FAMILY MINE
DIG IN!

"Let's go over the rules," their teacher, Mr Bracks, began. "Don't go near the mine entrance."

"If it caved in or collapsed, we could fall into the tunnel," Raj finished.

"That's right. And..."

"Stay together so no one gets lost," Raj added.

"Well, Raj has covered everything!" laughed Mr Bracks. "Today's dig will be exciting. You might find minerals, like gems, and other interesting stones. Any questions?"

Mia raised her hand. "Has someone really found a diamond here?"

"Yes! A big one, too," answered Mr Bracks. "It was a really unusual find for this area."

Ari gasped. "Was it from the lost treasure?"

"What treasure?" asked Jez.

"Long ago, two men robbed the Museum of Science," began Ari. "The police chased the robbers all over these hills. They finally caught them, right here at the mine!"

"That's just a story," said Raj. "Who knows if it is true? I'm not looking for made-up treasure."

"Raj does have a point," said Mr Bracks. "It turned out that diamonds had formed in this area."

Ari looked a bit sad hearing this news.

"However, a few years ago, someone dug up a ring," said Mr Bracks. "And the ring ended up belonging to the museum. So, how did it get here?"

No one answered.

Ari grinned, "I plan to find the missing treasure!"

Chapter Two
ROCK HOUNDS

"Welcome, rock hounds!" called the mine owner, Ms Torpie. The mine had been in her family for 100 years.

"What's a rock hound?" asked Jez.

"You!" laughed Ms Torpie. "It's someone who likes hunting for interesting rocks. Before you start, you'll need some tools."

"I brought my own!" said Raj. "My grandad sometimes takes me digging." He pulled everything out of his rucksack. "Shovel, bags to hold what we find, and a pickaxe for breaking big rocks. I also brought some goggles to protect me from the dust."

"Well, Raj has covered everything," laughed Mr Bracks. "Again!"

Raj grinned.

"I have tools and safety equipment for the rest of you," said Ms Torpie. "And when you have finished digging, you can bring back your finds for us to look at and study."

Ms Torpie pointed to a stream. "And one more thing," she said. "Scoop a bag of soil from that stream, too."

"Why?" asked Mia.

"The rarest stones usually form underground," explained Ms Torpie. "Moving water carries soil away to reveal or show those underground rocks that people find most valuable."

"Even diamonds?" asked Mia.

Shale   Coal   Chalk

"Not likely," Ms Torpie said as she held up a pencil. "In the past 100 years, only 13 have been found around here. See this pencil point? It started as a lump of coal. And so do diamonds. Diamonds just need MUCH more heat and pressure and a BILLION years to cook. Today, you may find stones that are more interesting than an old lump of coal."

Everyone laughed.

"Rocks are full of surprises," she said. "And sometimes, the hunt is worth more than the treasure."

Mia wondered what Ms Torpie meant as they headed out to dig.

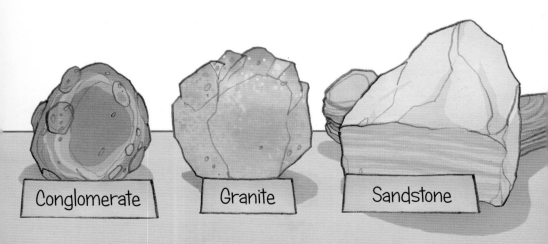

Conglomerate   Granite   Sandstone

Chapter Three
DIGGING FOR DIAMONDS

"Where shall we start?" asked Jez.

"Look at this app," said Mia, holding out her smartphone. It showed a map of the mine. She pointed to a spot. "We're here." She pointed to another spot dotted with flags. "The flags mean that interesting rocks were found in this spot. Let's go there."

Ari put his finger on the screen. "Let's go here."

"But nothing's been found there," said Mia.

"Mia's right," said Raj. "Most gems form near each other."

"Maybe my spot just hasn't been searched," said Ari. "Imagine what we might find?"

Jez agreed. "Let's dig at both places!"

That afternoon, four hot, dusty children headed from Mia's spot to Ari's. As they crossed the sunny meadow, the songs of crickets and blackbirds filled the air. The group was pleased to enter the cool, shady woods.

There was no path where they walked along the stream. Finally, Ari shouted, "Here!" They dropped their heavy bags and began working.

Tink! Tink! The rock picks struck.

Scratch, scoop! Shovels dug.

"Hey!" called Ari. "I've found something!" He washed it off in the stream.

Raj ran over. "It's just an old key."

"Yeah," said Ari. He threw it in his bag to look at later.

"I think we should head back now," shrugged Mia. "No diamonds for me today."

As they turned to leave, Jez stopped. "I almost forgot!" He dug his shovel into the stream, filling a bag with the heavy, wet soil. "Now let's go."

Chapter Four
ROCK STORIES

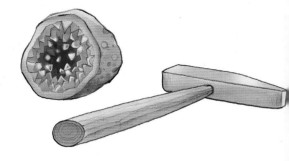

"Every rock tells a story," said Ms Torpie. She held a grey rock Mia had found. "What made you pick this?"

"I liked the round shape," said Mia.

"Watch as I hit it with a hammer," said Ms Torpie. Mia, Ari, Jez and Raj gave each other a confused look.

SLAM! The rock cracked down its middle. Ms Torpie handed it to Mia. "This rock has a secret," she whispered. "Open it." Inside was an empty, hollow space lined with rows of tiny purple crystals. They looked a little bit like purple glass.

"It's a geode," said Ms Torpie. "A great find!"

The children took turns passing it around.

Mia smiled. It was a great find. And just as pretty as a diamond!

Ms Torpie picked up Raj's find. "How about this one?" she asked, holding up a long, smooth, barrel-shaped stone.

"I picked that one," said Raj. "It was so much heavier than I thought it would be. It feels as though someone has filled it up with metal or something."

Ms Torpie passed it around. "It's definitely heavy, but it's not a rock. It's part of a tree," said Ms Torpie. "Or rather, it used to be part of a tree. It's called petrified wood. It's wood that has hardened into something like rock. It's a fossil now."

"Cool!" whispered Jez.

"A fossil is a sign of life long ago," said Ms Torpie. "This fossil is from a tree that lived more than a million years ago. You can see the patterns of bark on its outside, and the rings on its inside."

"How did it form?" asked Ari.

"It started when the tree died and fell to the ground. As the insides rotted, mud soaked in through cracks in the bark," explained Ms Torpie. "Then, the minerals in the mud hardened. These minerals are what gives the wood all those colours."
She handed it back to Raj.

"Wow!" said Mia.

Raj couldn't believe his luck! He smiled, rubbing his thumb along the wood's ridges.

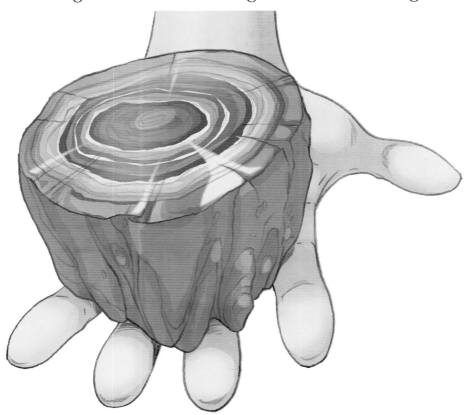

Chapter Five
LOST AND FOUND

Next Ms Torpie shook the stream soil Jez brought back into a special pan. The sand fell through tiny holes in its bottom, leaving the larger stones on top.

"Let's look at these," said Ms Torpie. She washed off the stones.

Suddenly, she gasped. "An opal!" She held up a stone that was smoky black, yet filled with colour. "Opals don't form here. And this one has been cut and polished! It's smooth and perfectly shaped."

"Then how…?" said Raj.

"The treasure!" said Ari hopefully.

"The lost museum treasure? After all this time?" said Ms Torpie.

"I found a key near that spot, too!" Ari handed it to her. "Is it possible it could open a treasure chest?"

Ms Torpie took the key from Ari. "When I was a child, everyone believed the legend of the lost treasure," she said. "Do you remember it, Mr Bracks?"

"I might have searched these woods looking for it myself," he said.

"I'll tell you why that key excites me," said Ms Torpie. "Even in prison, the thieves never told anyone where to find the treasure. Instead, they argued about two things. The first was who to blame for getting caught."

"And the second?" asked Ari.

"WHO LOST THE KEY."

Everyone fell silent.

"We thought the thieves buried the treasure around here and that they lost the key while running from the police." Now she looked closely at the key. "Wait! There's writing!"

"Pine Mountain Bank, Number 31," read Ms Torpie. She sighed. "This won't unlock a buried treasure chest."

"It unlocks a box at a bank," explained Mr Bracks. "Sorry, kids."

"What if the robbers didn't bury the treasure? What if they put it in a very safe place, like a bank!" asked Raj. "But where is that bank? I've never heard of it."

"Here," Mia said, looking at her smartphone. "This says Pine Mountain Bank burned down in 1910."

"That's more than 100 years ago!" cried Ari.

Mia grinned. "Good news! The boxes were in a vault. A vault is a metal room that's safe from fire," she said. Then she added, "The bank boxes were all moved to the museum! They're part of an exhibit showing our town's past."

"Let's go to the…" But before Mr Bracks could finish, everyone was already on their way out of the door.

Chapter Six
ROCK STAR!

"I can't believe this!" said Ms Francis, the museum director. She quickly led them down a long corridor until they reached the bank display. "I've never opened the boxes. They've been here so long, I thought anything inside had already been removed." She stopped. "Here it is! Box 31!" she called.

Ari gulped as he put the key in the lock. Would it work?

Click! The box popped open.

A glow radiated from the small box. It was the glow from one very large diamond.

"You've FOUND it, Ari! The treasure!" Mia shouted. She nearly tripped over her feet to see the diamond. The box also held four more keys with numbers on them.

Ari handed one to each friend. "Ready?" he said. "Set? Open!" More light spilled out from the boxes. They were filled with sparkling metals of gold and silver and rare stones of all colours.

"All these years," said Ms Francis. "The stolen treasure was where it belonged!"

Mia raised her hand. "Can Ari keep all the treasure?" asked Mia. "He was the one who found the key, after all."

"It **is** Finders Keepers at the Torpie Family Mine," said Ms Torpie. "But in this case…"

Ari held up a hand to stop her. "I wouldn't dream of keeping the treasure, even if I could. It belongs here, of course."

"Sometimes, the hunt is worth more than the treasure. Isn't that right, Ms Torpie?" Ari asked smiling. He was holding up a red stone from one of the boxes.

"That's right, Ari," she smiled.

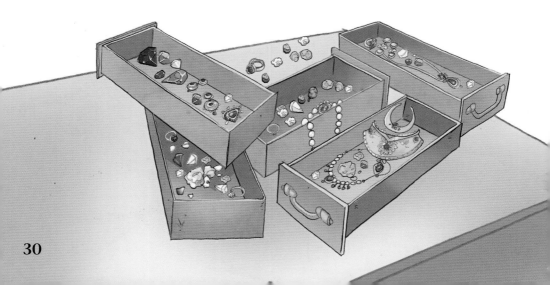